Little Stories of Great

THAT'S MY PIANO, SIR!

WOLFGANG AMADEUS MOZART

Story Ana Gerhard Illustrations Marie Lafrance
Musical Recordings I Musici de Montréal
Narration Colm Feore

Hi, my name is Minim. In my family, we love cheese and music, although I couldn't tell you which comes first. What I can tell you is that we have a gift —or an ear—for finding great music.

The boat is late this evening, which has put everyone in a lousy mood. The dockworkers are gloomy because they won't be home in time for supper. "Worse yet, it's freezing cold," grumbles the customs officer, rubbing his arms to try and stay warm.

And what about us mice? We are desperate for everyone to leave so that we can finally come out of our holes, take in the fresh air, run around, play a few games, and look for something to eat.

Finally, a horn sounds announcing the boat's arrival. Everyone on the dock impatiently gets into action. As soon as the boat is securely moored, the dockworkers begin unloading luggage. The passengers are slow to disembark, however, as they have to wait in line to clear customs. Their sullen faces leave no doubt that they are just as cold and hungry as we are.

My head is exploding with anticipation! My mouth waters at the thought of all the succulent food waiting to be devoured! There will be leftover cake and cheese, fruit, sauces— everything the passengers haven't eaten will be taken to the back of the boat to be thrown into large waste bins. A little patience and the feast will be all ours!

Unfortunately, a great deal of luggage still remains on the deck, and the line of passengers appears to go on forever.

Suddenly the delicious aroma of Roquefort (my favourite cheese!) comes wafting through the air. Unable to resist a moment longer, I follow my nose out of my hiding spot. Intent only on finding the cheese, I don't notice two strapping fellows approach with an enormous crate.

I'm just about to be crushed when one of them spots me. Startled, he loses his footing and falls backwards.

The crate lands on him with a crash, and a strange sound comes ringing through the cold evening air. In the ensuing confusion, I scamper to safety as quickly as I can.

Straightaway, I see a young lad push his way to the crate through the gathering crowd of curious bystanders. This is no ordinary boy! Sporting a white wig, elegantly dressed in red velvet and clutching a strange little case, he looks like a character from a fairy tale.

"I knew I heard it," he says with a smile on his face. He turns politely and enquires of the dockworker, still shaken from his fall, "Are you alright, my good man? Are you hurt?"
"No," mutters the man as he gets up. "I'm all right, thanks."

Drawn by all the racket, the customs officer comes over, followed by another man and a young girl, both dressed as stylishly as the boy. The man seems quite displeased! Without waiting to be scolded, the two workers quickly set the crate straight. Miraculously, it does not appear to have been damaged in the fall.

The boy takes a key from his pocket and immediately opens the lid. To everyone's surprise, the crate turns into a piano.

It's most peculiar to see such an instrument standing in the middle of a dock! The customs officer, who clearly has had a very long day, only manages to stammer, "Who would have such a ludicrous idea?"

The elegant older man is about to respond when the clear
voice of the boy proudly affirms, "That's my piano, sir!
We are travelling with it because my sister and I are playing
several concerts here in the city and we need to practise.
I also have my violin with me."

He opens the case, takes out a violin and proudly shows it
to the customs officer, who is still speechless with surprise.

The boy takes a moment to tune the violin and then gives a knowing glance to his sister, Nannerl, who approaches the piano. The two children begin to play together.

The cold and fatigue are soon forgotten as everyone's spirits rise almost magically. After the music, life returns to normal: travellers get into line, the customs officer goes back to his duties, and the hustle and bustle resumes on the dock. Yet somehow, everything has changed. The evening air now seems to glisten, and people's faces are beaming.

That night, I sleep like an angel, my belly full of Roquefort and my ears ringing with music.

I didn't realize at the time that the little lad on the dock whose music had brightened a weary day was none other than Wolfgang Amadeus Mozart—one of the greatest composers of all time.

A FEW MORSELS OF HISTORY

Wolfgang Amadeus Mozart (1756–1791) was a composer of the Classical period. He wrote many works and excelled in every musical form of the time. His name became synonymous with genius, virtuosity and musical excellence.

Born into a family of musicians, from the tender age of three little Wolfgang ("Wolfer" to his family) sought out notes that "went well together" on sister Nannerl's piano. He quickly displayed an astonishing musical talent and began composing minuets around the age of five. His father, Leopold, saw to his son's musical education. Aware of his son's precocious and exceptional talent, he organized endless trips to put him on display at European courts.

One of the earliest of these trips took them along the Danube by boat to Vienna, where young Wolfgang was to play for the Empress Maria Theresa and her family. In a letter, Leopold recounted his son's success in playing piano and violin upon landing in Vienna. Wolfgang was just six at the time.

Mozart's first four *Sonatas for piano and violin (KV 6–9)* were composed between 1762 and 1764. Over the course of his life, Mozart would go on to write 36 sonatas for violin and piano. *The Little Night Music K525* composed 25 years later is one of the summits of classical music.

Story Ana Gerhard Illustrations Marie Lafrance Musical Recordings Orchestre de chambre I Musici de Montréal
Musical Director Jean-Marie Zeitouni Narration Colm Feore Producer Carl Talbot
Musicians recorded at Concordia University's Oscar Peterson Concert Hall Christopher Johns
assisted by Philippe Bouvrette Narrator recorded at Fred Smith Studio Fred Smith and Max Smith
Additional recordings and mixing Productions Musicom inc. Sound effects Eric Lemoyne
Sound editing Philippe Bouvrette Mastering at Le Lab Mastering Marc Thériault Artistic Director Roland Stringer
Graphic design Stephan Lorti for Haus Design Original French editing Janou Gagnon
Translation Services d'édition Guy Connolly Copy editing Ruth Joseph for Tangerine Media

The narrated story includes the recordings *The Little Night Music K.525, 4th Movement*
and *Sonata for piano and violin KV.8, 1st Movement*.

Musicians

Concertmaster Julie Triquet Violins Amélie Benoit Bastien, Denis Béliveau, Dominic Guilbault,
Annie Guénette, Madeleine Messier, Marie-Ève Poupart, Christian Prévost and Hubert Brizard
Violas Anne Beaudry, Suzanne Careau and Jacques Proulx Cellos Alain Aubut, Tim Halliday and Carla Antoun
Double Bass Yannick Chênevert Oboes Kirsten Zander and Marjorie Tremblay
Horns Louis-Philippe Marsolais and Simon Bourget Harpsichord Christophe Gauthier
Piano Gaspard Tanguay-Labrosse

Julie Triquet plays a Giuseppe Odoardi 1786 violin generously loaned by Mr. David B. Sela
Amélie Benoit Bastien plays a Romano Marengo Rinaldi 1898 violin generously loaned by CANIMEX
Annie Guénette plays a Joseph Gagliano 1768 violin generously loaned by CANIMEX
Tim Halliday plays a Mira Gruszow and Gideon Baumblatt's Kolia cello (2014),
generously loaned by Mr. David B. Sela

I Musici de Montréal Administration
Executive Director **Marisol de Santis**
Associate Director, Marketing, Communications and Sales **Anna Bedic**
Manager, Finance and Administration **Volha Laiter**

Acknowledgements

**Edna Khubyar, Simon Gamache, Pierre-Marie Audard, Carole Therrien,
Thérèse Boutin** and **Marie-Luce Gervais**

A unique code for the digital download of the recordings of the narrated story and the performance of *A Little Night Music* ("Eine Kleine Nachtmusik") along with a printable file of the illustrated story is also included.

Ⓟ Ⓒ 2020 The Secret Mountain (Folle Avoine Productions)
ISBN 13: 978-2-924774-82-3 / ISBN 10: 2-924774-82-9
Ⓡ www.thesecretmountain.com